This book belongs to:

_____

The Frog from the Bog
Published 2021 Frog Light Press

Text and illustration copyright © 2021 by Rebecca Kwait

Library of Congress Catalog Card Number pending.

First edition 2021.

ISBN: 978-0-578-93923-0

Frog Light Press

The Frog
from the Bog

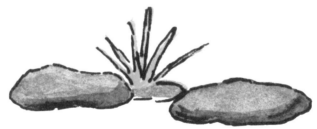

Written and Illustrated

by

Rebecca Kwait

For Dylan, Aiden and Adeline.
And Sam, for all of your help, xo.

Samson the frog,
was tired of living in a bog.
And yearned
for a warm bed of straw.

His home was green,
and the farm next door so pristine!

So, he thought,
"Why not go on a tour?!"

All the other frogs thought he was crazy.

But honestly they were quite lazy.

And they told him he would never fit in.

"But how could they know?" wondered Samson,
"When none of them have ever been!"

"To them I might be strange, slippery and green.
An amphibian, farm animals have never seen."

"But I am lovable and kind!"
"So perhaps they won't mind?"

So off he did hop from rock to rock,
until he bounced up a grassy knoll.

Down to the farm yard, he crashed through the gate.

To the surprise of three ducks and a cat.

"Wow! I love this place already!" thought Samson,

"You think I can stay here?" he said to a friendly looking rat.

"My name's Earl" said the rat,
"What on earth are you?"

"Why, a frog!" Samson replied.

"A frog you say! Well, you made my day!"
Earl rolled over and cried.

"Can I ask what you are?" Samson slowly said.
"Oh! I am the farm lookout!" Earl replied, lifting up his head.

"Foxes sometimes slink around to steal eggs at night."

"I sniff them out, wake the dog, and turn on the light!
The farm animals love me, even though I'm a rat.
And my job is super important, I've got it down pat!"

"I like you!" said Samson. "Life here sounds great!"

To meet all of the other animals, Samson could hardly wait!

The two became fast friends,
even though quite an odd pair.
Earl showed Samson the barn and said,
"You can sleep here!"

It was exactly as Samson had imagined, cozy, warm and dry.

A lofty, friendly place, with chickens, horses, pigs and a....

Fly !

Earl however apologized and said,
"Sorry for the flies! They can be pesky!"

But then Samson showed what he could do...

And gobbled **TEN** flies before you could say

"TWO!"

Cried Earl in disbelief.
Then Samson smiled a smile of relief.

All the animals LOVED having
Samson on the farm!
Without one thousand flies,
they were all much more calm!

They even gave him a bucket to swim in from time to time.
Just in case he wanted to get wet and moisten his slime.

Who knew that a little green frog could fit right in, amongst animals big and small.

A new friend is a wonderful gift.
Looks don't matter at all!

The End

Meet the Author

Rebecca Kwait is a first time children's book author and illustrator. Born and raised in Trinidad, a beautiful, multi-cultural, Caribbean nation, she came to the US during medical school and ultimately became a breast cancer surgeon. As a mother of small children, she often dreamed of writing and illustrating a children's book and fantasized that the story could have an important message.

During a very challenging 2020, with the support of her wonderful family, Samson was created. A small creature with big dreams to overcome the impossible. His story teaches us an important lesson about inclusion: While someone may be different, accept them for who they are and you might be surprised by how much good they can bring to the world.

Rebecca currently lives in Marblehead, Massachusetts.

CPSIA information can be obtained
at www.ICGtesting.com
Printed in the USA
BVHW061745221122
652525BV00010B/794